BETHANY NEVER

BY

JACKIE SWIFT

W0006749

LIMITED EDITION
OF 100

FAHRENHEIT PRESS

BETHANY TYLER – POLITICAL PROVOCATEUR OR PRECOCIOUS PRINCESS?

An exclusive expose by Jasper Rocca for the Inside Inquirer

Recent events have rocked the national capital and indeed the nation. Prime Minister, Howard Johnson, was attacked and seriouly injured by teenage school-girl, Bethany Tyler, at an event at Government House held as the finale to the annual National Youth Parliament. While the Prime Minister hovers between life and death, serious questions have been rasied about how this happened. How did this young woman evade the security measures in place at Government House? How did she smuggle weapons into the building and how was she able to get close enough to Mr Johnson to inflict life threatening injuries?

Much has been written in this paper and elsewhere about the track record of the current Prime Minister and his government; much of it laudable but some matters which have clearly caused wide-spread discontent and angry criticism in the community. However, while as a country we have a history of protest and dissent, we do not have a history of violence, especially not towards

our elected officials. Until last week we
had no instances of anyone attempting to maim
or assassinate the country's leader. This is
not America: we do not kill our presidents.
We do not carry guns as a matter of course.
Our leaders have been confident when
mingling with the public, either out and
about or at functions where people are
pleased to be invited and abide by the
relevant protocols.

The actions of Bethany Tyler in attacking
Howard Johnson, a democratically elected
official, have opened deep fissures in our
society, forcing some unpalatable questions
to be asked. The main one being: how have we
come to this, that a schoolgirl, a teenager
from a good family who attends an excellent
school, has become so radicalised as to
attempt to take the life of the Prime
Minister?

As part of this paper's examination of this
issue I have interviewed key people related
to Bethany Tyler to see if we can unlock what
led this young woman to partake in an act of
unprovoked violence. Here is your
opportunity to hear from those closest to
Bethany Tyler, to see if we can understand
how this terrible event came to pass.

Grace Tyler

Bethany really was a very ordinary girl. *Was*
– heavens, I'm speaking about her in the past
tense, as if she no longer exists. I don't
mean that, I mean, she clearly isn't the girl
we thought she was. She was a normal, sweet,

ordinary child. She was gorgeous as a baby, as most babies are, especially to their parents. She met all her developmental landmarks without any effort, was slightly ahead in terms of length for a while – all limbs and things, a very active child. A happy child I would say. There was nothing to indicate that anything unusual or unexpected would happen. See, look at this picture – just a pretty little girl. Would you like that, for your paper? So, you can imagine our surprise when the call came to tell us what had happened. I simply didn't believe it. But it was on all the news channels. Bethany, clear as day being taken into custody – glorious in her school uniform. I bet they had kittens watching that, their precious school connected to one of the biggest political stories in history. I know Roger was stunned. Not his little girl, not his princess. And she was certainly that. I guess if Will was my golden haired boy then Bethany was Daddy's indulged girl. Well, why have a daughter and not spoil her? That was Roger's reasoning.

I feel I should have sensed something was up. Mothers are meant to know their children best, aren't they? I mean I knew Will would join the Air Force – even with that incredible HSC score, he wasn't doing Medicine for anything. He'd always wanted to be an astronaut, and the accepted pathway is to be a pilot with the Forces and then head to NASA. No amount of bribery or coercion from Roger was going to dissuade him, not after Will got the Defence Forces scholarship in year 11.

How could a son of mine even contemplate joining such an institution? Roger had railed. *Not under this reactionary, war-mongering government. He'll end up in bloody Iraq. This war's going forever- you watch. Bugger bloody NASA. Your son won't live long enough!*

Will had stormed out of the room, as he was wont to do with his dad. And there was Bethany, bless her, who ran and got Roger a glass of red and sat him down and filled his head with the frothy, amusing details of her day. By the end of the glass she'd wheedled a weekend shopping in Melbourne for her and Sasha staying at the Hyatt. I'd sat with Will, letting him fume and let off steam, calling his dad all sorts of terrible, if not true, things. What Roger never understood about Will was how single minded he was. He'd decided on his career path when he was in primary school, everything else was somehow to do with being part of the Space business. His obsession with fitness, his buidling projects (so much Lego as a boy!), his keen understanding of computers and anything tech. It was obvious from the time he saw that film with Tom Hanks that Space was the only choice. Never Medicine, he was never going to be a doctor. I don't know why Roger persisted – buying into the trope that all clever people must become doctors. If anyone was going to obssess about things, get steamed up enough to act, it was Will; logical, clever, clincal. A boy with a plan. Now I could see Will doing what Beth did. I really could.

No wonder we didn't see this coming. All

Beth cared about was shopping, clothes, music and her increasing social life. She cared deeply about superficial things. It's true, I found her hard to deal with: Roger was so much better with her. Even as a little girl. I found her obsession with trivial matters – dolls then clothes and hair, and always parties – far too wearing. How many conversations could you have about Barbie and the latest incarnation or accessories? How many new outfits did one little girl need? Every new party, and she was a very popular person, meant a new outfit. She was exactly the sort of person that led to the state the planet is now in. New, new new. Never recycled, never anything from an Op Shop or the lovely little antique shops that are all over the place. She wouldn't even wander into one just to have a look. What happens if her friends saw her in those sorts of shops? I tried doing practical things with her; cooking, some gardening, so she she could learn some usefull skills and gain some understanding about how the planet worked. That we didn't need to madly consume all the time; that home baking and growing your own vegetables, as well having chickens was a good thing to do, for us and for generations to come. She grew one strawberry plant and baked a decent batch of cup-cakes but lost interest very quickly. We didn't even get to tomatoes or home relish or jam making.

But she could get away with anything with Roger. Bethany never did anything wrong. Daddy's little angel. She takes him cups of tea in his study, fetches his bits and pieces from where-ever he'd left them in the house so he could work uninterupted. She'd make him a sandwhich whenever he wanted. She didn't see that she was such a cliché, and God knows, Roger didn't say anything, just soaked up the devotion. He never minded all her toys and clothes and the need for the latest whatever it was. He just shrugged and smiled and said *why not*? He earned enough money and surely the point of money was to be able to buy things for those you loved? He'll be like that now. Muster all the legal advice in the world and find some excuse for this not being her fault.

But, let's be clear, young man, she *had* changed recently, she wasn't that superficial girl focused on herself and her friends and all things celebrity and ephemeral. Something shifted in her, I don't know why or how. We really weren't a chatty, sharing mother and daughter. Don't get me wrong, I love Beth, I've just never really understood her. She's been like some foundling to me most of her life. Obviously mine – as you look at her, the genes are strong – but her character, her interests were so opposite to mine, right from the start, so we've never had a close connection. So no, I wasn't privy to her thoughts and ideas: I hadn't the first idea how much was changing.

She'd started doing volunteer work at the Greens' office and she was right into that Youth Parliament thing. Not because of us. Absolutely not. She was dismissive of my work and Roger's pro-bono efforts. *Is that Bono's half brother?* And she was developing a real interest in the proposed Pulp Mill. She came to the rallies with us, something she'd done as a baby, back when she had no choice. But once she had a choice she'd begged off. Will still came along but not Beth. So that was a sudden and unexpected change. Roger and I spoke about it but essentially we were just happy to see her becoming more altruistic, less self obsessed. I did wonder if it was some sort of passing phase, something to do with one of her friends, or a boy even. It seemed more likely to be to do with someone else and she was ripe for love, so I was quite sure it was connected to a male of some description, someone she wanted to impress. I know that sounds harsh, but Beth, up until recent months simply wasn't interested in much beyond herself. She really wasn't. She was just a normal egocentric teenager. But I've always loved her. You love your children. No matter what.

You must understand – Roger and I are very proud of Bethany. She's taken a hard decision and she'll pay a very high price but principles can't be bought cheaply. I just hope it was worth it. No matter what happens to Johnson, we'll stand by Beth.

Roger Tyler

As I think back on Bethany's life I'd have to say that we under-estimated her. She was a sweet and easy baby. Walked at the right time, talked when she was meant to. Said *Dad* first – all that stuff. A very normal baby. Grace will agree. Will was the one we expected great things of. Still do, he's only just beginning his life. Doing very well in the Air Force. Loves it up there in the air. I think he's looking at Intelligence: well, they wanted him to consider it. I guess that's all stuffed now, though. Still, Beth's stunt shouldn't hurt his NASA chances: America cares very little about our political shenanigans: look at history, current politics – we really don't rate on the world stage. Besides it'll be a very different political world by the time Will makes the move to the USA. I'm sure this will all blow over. I'm sure Johnson will be just fine and we'll see this for what it is, an abberation by a naïve young girl influenced by a much older man.

Anyway, Beth was a compliant child. Very much a girl's girl and, yes, Grace is right, Daddy's girl. I don't think there's a problem with that. Beth has always been a sweet girl. There's nothing bitchy or underhand in her. She may have driven Grace mad with her Barbies and need for brand items, but in the scheme of things it really didn't matter. Beth was easy to live with, she was always polite, always appreciative of anything bought or done for her; always a ready smile on her face. She mucked in with chores around the house, helped in the garden, and was considerate of others. I don't think she was spoilt. She didn't like the things that Grace liked; she wasn't a great reader, she didn't push herself at school, but she did all right. She had no idea about what she was going to do with her life. But she had time. Just because Will has been so single minded since he was ten didn't mean Beth had to have her life mapped out as well. Over the last couple of years I could see why Grace was worried about Beth's lack of ambition or direction. Where would she end up? I couldn't see her at Uni – what would she do there? And even though I never said a word to Grace, I wasn't keen on paying for university if Beth was just going to spend a few years doing nothing in particular except look for a husband, ending up with a BA that led absolutely nowhere. Perhaps some other sort of course? But her lack of interests and skills was starting to bother me. No, I didn't share those concerns with Grace. I wasn't going to give her a chance to say *I told you so*. I kept my worries about Beth strictly to myself.

Of course I was going to send her to that school when she asked. Will didn't need any special attention. He didn't need anything extra to keep him on track, to get him where he wanted to go. A private school would have made no difference to him. But it meant a great deal to Bethany. Her girlfriends, her best friends, all of them, were going there. How could she go anywhere else? Besides, as I think now – with the benefit of hind-sight – perhaps I thought it was exactly the right school for Beth. A strong academic record, a rich and varied cultural and sporting program, high expectations, a strong peer group. Perhaps it was just what Beth needed to move her along, to give her some ambition, to make something of herself. Yes, perhaps those niggling worries about her were in me even when she was twelve, even if I hadn't consciously realised it. No father, not these days, wants a daughter who can't take care of herself, who can't live an independent life. That would make me a failure as a parent. I wasn't intending on spoiling Bethany to that extent. No, the school would help her find who she was, what she wanted to do. I believed that then. Even if I'm not sure now.

Grace said we were indulging Beth, that if the government system had been good enough for us and for Will, then why wasn't it good enough for her? Did we really want Will to think that Bethany meant more to us?

There was no logical reason to deny Beth's request about the school, despite Grace's heavy play to the emotions and perceived unfairness to Will. The practise was thriving: there was no financial reason to deny Beth. Grace had her new Jag. We bought Will a car as he turned 17; we continue to support him financially, so that he doesn't have to work part-time to supplement his scholarship. It wasn't all Beth and nobody else. It's easy for Grace to get confused. I know she works hard for her volunteer organizations, but I bankroll a lot of what goes on. A great many of her immigration causes would have been lost without all the work the practice's done over the years. But look, that's the right thing to do. We should give back to our community and the world at large. Wealthy nations like Australia owe it to the poorer countries. It's true, we in the West, simply do not do enough for developing nations. And we really need to step up in our obligations to the environment. It's more than saving rivers and Old Growth Forests nowadays, it's the whole planet in crisis.

So, if you think about it logically, Beth
has been surrounded by left wing Green
politics all her life. She started
volunteering at Michael Porter's office,
came along to the rallies with us again.
Grace thinks she was there because of Michael
Porter. But Beth chose to get involved in
the Youth Parliament: we didn't push it. So
I think it was a mark of Beth's developing
social conscience, enhanced by the
opportunities that the school offered. How
could she not have one with Grace as her
mother? Beth's been surrounded by worthy
causes all her life. Why not accept that Beth
has matured into her own political being and
has taken a brave, if somewhat foolish,
stand?

Will Tyler

I thought I knew my sister. Vain,
superficial, into hair straighteners, lip
gloss from the Body Shop, Bath bombs from
Lush anytime Mum went to Sydney, all that
reality TV shit, plus a string of boys always
messaging her. She was completely disdainful
of me, Mum and anything that put her at odds
with the thought police that masqueraded as
her gaggle of equally superficial friends.
Only Dad was fooled by those Animae eyes and
that quivering pout. Mum sort of knew what
she was up to, but Roge was hood-winked all
the time. Beth had some powerful line in
bullshit. I don't think he had the faintest
clue. Too many parties and far more alcohol
than I've ever ingested. She'd always been

a party girl, but parties in primary school are a whole different ball-game in secondary school. She got away with murder there: so many sleep-overs at the elegant homes of respectable families. I could only wonder what the other parents thought was happening at those parties. To be honest, I'm amazed nothing disastrous happened at them.

School for Beth was about socialising, making connections, it was not at all about the stuff Roge thought it was going to be about. Not much academic rigor for Beth, bugger all cultural challenge – she spent years miming the flute during concerts (I can only wonder what she did in music lessons…) and several seasons of embarassing netball. She could have been okay, if she'd had a go. But Roge never saw the lack of effort, only his girl braving the winter rain and fog out there every Saturday morning, losing graciously nearly every week. Although perhaps for people like Beth connections are what matters and so she was in the right place, despite Grace's vehement protestations.

I must admit though, recent events have blown me away. I mean, you're here to get some sort of insight I guess. Run some insider scoop on the girl who… and because…

I can't help you much. Before I left home – I've been gone for three years now – she was an air head, no future plans except some version of life that could only ever lead to disaster as all her values and expectations were based on trivial American soap operas and that snobby vacuous lot at that precious school of hers. Did Roger really not understand the importance of the peer group: that no school, no matter how glossy and glowing its prospectus, can counter the peer group?

Now *that* caused the worst argument between Mum and Dad. Grace was livid. Her life long support of public education, of social justice all destroyed in one indulgent swoop. How could she face her friends? How could she retain any credibility or dignity? Didn't Roger understand that? Where was his radical soul, his protestor past? How could he let his daughter loose in the house of the enemy, in the bastion of privilege and old school ties?

Grace's bile was countered by Roger's superior argument that pointed out the facts:

- She, Grace, was only able to indulge her leftie, compassionate politics because he, Roger worked like a dog and had done for years while she stayed home: at first with the children, which, yes, he had wanted too, and then because she wanted to give back to society, not through working as a teacher, as she was trained, but through volunteer work (she'd gotten a taste for unpaid work at uni being on a range of protest organising committees in her time)

- He, Roger, paid all the bills and if Beth wanted to go to *that* school then she could

- She, Grace, had very happily accepted a brand new V8 Jaguar (complete with cream leather interiors and bespoke

metalic maroon paintwork) for her
birthday without that upsetting her
credibility or dignity

- He, Roger, gave a great deal of
support, both financial and personal
to her worthy causes and helped her
credibility and status on a tangible
basis

- And, he, Roger, was not going to
indulge her, Grace's, petulance;
besides, Bethany might learn some
unexpected things at the school, get a
broader view of the world, and that,
he said, conclusively, wouldn't be such
a bad thing.

Mum sulked for a few days and Roger worked
late at his office but finally took her out
to dinner to make up for reducing her to
tears and being so blunt. In the meantime
Beth had her mobile up-graded and her ears
pierced again – all courtesy of Roge. I might
have got some money for nothing so I'm not
actually complaining, just trying to give
you some idea of how home was. Mum, the uber
compassion queen of good works; Dad, the
leftie lawyer; me, the boy-genius and
Bethany the princess. Not that unusual
really.

So, you can see that while our family
situation would seem conductive to such
extreme political actions, especially given
Grace and Roger's status in the Green
political community, none of us would have
pointed to Beth. Grace, yes, given the
opportunity. Roger would have when younger;
not now, far too straight and respectable

and I've just never been political, much to
Grace's eternal disappointment, which she
does her best to hide. For all Grace's good
works, Beth may well have had the biggest
single impact on Oz politics for years. Well
since The Dismissal. Too young for all that
but it's one of those commemorated annual
events in the house of Tyler.

Remember, Remember
the 11th November
forever and ever.

So, in my humble opinion, years of the home
political environment finally seeped into
her consciousness: you can't attend
political rallies and protests as a child
and be around political people (all our
family friends are of the Green persuasion
and spend their time in good works; some are
politicans and all of them have spend hours
at our place in heated debates and long
lunches) without some impact. I mean, I'm
not an activist but I genuinely of my own
free will up-hold my parents' political
views, even if in an entirely private way.
  Plus, something at *that* school triggered
it. There would have to have been an external
reason – Beth doesn't have any initiative of
her own. Or real brains for that matter, and
it was a very well executed act. You've got
to admit that. I believe Sasha Coleman was
the trigger. A friendship from primary
school that was forged into something quite
special at *that* school. A girl I'd never
really liked. A pretty girl with a devious
mouth.

Talk to Sasha - you'll get some answers.

Sasha Coleman

Obviously, I'm as shocked as anyone. You have to believe that. While we may have talked about direct action in class and as part of the broader political conversations we were having, we wouldn't *do* anything radical. That was never part of the agenda. And I just could never *do* anything like that. I mean, in all those discussions I never *said* anything about *doing* anything. Daddy wasn't happy about me being involved in the whole Youth Parliament thing anyway. And you can imagine what he's saying now. No, don't ask him what he thinks of Bethany and her family. Not after this! I'll be lucky if I ever see her again. If she *ever* gets out.

You want to know how it started, what triggered Beth into action, what was it that changed this perfectly normal school-girl into a violent activist. And why I've remained unscathed, removed from such terrible-terible action while my best friend succumbed. You want to know how a girl from a school with such an impeccable reputation could do this…

I know, it's just awful, isnt it? And I wonder, I really do, if *I* could have stopped her? If only *I'd* been paying closer attention to Beth, could *I* have done anything? Honestly, I'm losing sleep, worrying about her, wondering every day what *I* could have done differently.

So, it all began with *increasing our awareness of the plight of others*. We were getting ready for one of our charity things, where we raise money for those worse off than us. We were searching around for something meaningful to support, to do. Not just fun-runs, or 24 hours on the oval existing on rice and an apple. Anyway, one of the local MPs was just fabulous when he came into school. He was all passion and shiny hair, knew so much about the entire scene – you know, what was really going on in the forests and the immigration and detainee thing. He'd been to the Baxter Detention Centre. Seen their mouths sewn up. Had all these gruesome photos.

I think that's what got to Beth. I mean her mum's into it all. How many letters does that woman write to the papers? She must be on some ASIO list of subversive loonies. Well, Daddy says she is. But it didn't mean anything to Beth until she met Michael and well, let's face it, fell for him. I mean, he was entirely *hot*, and Beth was completely *ga-ga*. He could have told her anything and she'd have believed him. She'd have done *anything* for him. Perhaps this thing with the PM was all his idea? You know, that could be likely. There you go, a lead.

Anyway, if we're looking for blame, I guess it was Mrs Johansen's fault. She runs Youth Parliament at school. She invited Michael Porter in to speak to us about the importance of voting, etc, etc, as well as inspire us about our charity efforts. You could see the impact on Beth. She was all fired about about the detention centres, couldn't shut up about them and how to raise awareness and money for them. Then as soon as Beth realised

Michael was going to be part of the whole YP scene, she was in. I could see it in her eyes: nothing to do with altruistic pursuits, not becoming *her mother's child after all*, as Mrs Johansen gushed when Beth signed up, dragging me with here.

Honestly, you need to speak to Mrs Johansen. She stirred it all up. If she hadn't invited Michael Porter into the school, if he hadn't spoken so well, if he hadn't offered to help out with the Youth Parliament then Beth would have eaten rice on the oval, worn a slogan covered flourescent t-short for a weekend, shouted slogans and waved placarts for the required time with the rest of us and got over it all. She'd have done her bit for charity and everything would have been fine. But no, Mrs Johansen brought Michael Porter into the school and let him bewitch Bethany so that she wasn't herself anymore at all.

I think, you know, that I went along with her to keep her safe. I think I had an idea that Michael Porter was trouble. I could see that Bethany was lost and needed someone to try and save her. I tried to save her. I really did.

Anyway, we got our Bills to prepare. One on the detainees, one on the forestry industry, and how handy, Michael Porter had all this information that we could use, plus he was more than willing to help, to give up his own time for us. Beth got *so* excited about social justice: how we needed to be a more compassionate society. She got way too serious if you asked me. And way too boring about it. But I'm her friend and I stuck with her, as best friends should.

But she just spent more and more time at Michael's office; after school and weekends doing electoral things for him. Making his coffee, licking his stamps, stuffing his envelopes. I went along for a bit, but it was clear she didn't really want me there. And who wants to spent their Saturdays helping some boring politician? And she talked about nothing else. About how clever he was, how much good he was doing. Then she met Benny Black, Emperor of the Greens, King of Protestors and Saviour of the Forests, had a conversation with him, all earnest and meaningful, and I swear she just wasn't the same person. I mean, she must have met him before with her parents, but somehow this time was different. He spoke to her, listened to her. So, it was like Jesus had touched her. She was *saved*, if you get my meaning. She wouldn't even come down the Mall with me anymore and the others dropped her. But she didn't seem to care. I hung in, hoping she'd be fine again once we'd been to Canberra, done our YP thing and came home. She'd forget about Michael Porter and be her old self.

I mean her parents *must* have noticed the difference. She just gushed Green politics all the time. You know *Michael says,* on everything on the planet. Then she went to the Pulp Mill rallies with Green Grace and Radical Roge without complaining, so unless they are as up themselves as she says, they must have noticed. So, they can't be surprised by this and they can't blame me. Nobody can.

Especially not when Daddy drew the line at

the rallies. He put his foot down there. No way was a man in his position (you know who he is) going to allow his only daughter to be seen at such politically dangerous (to him) events. He nearly stopped me going to Canberra, but I managed to perusade him that I needed to be there, that I'd be letting the school down to suddenly withdraw. I didn't mention my need to be close to Bethany, that I was worried about her. No, that wouldn't have made Daddy happy. It's not that he dislikes Bethany, well, he didn't before now, he didn't even mind who her parents were. But now everything is different, isnt it? But he understands public service, so I played that card. Daddy relented then: he's big on reputation and loyalty. He went to the school too, and is terribly upset about everything; the damage to the school, the political fall-out – what if Howard Johnson dies?

So as well as looking at Mrs Johansen's role in this, in throwing Beth and Michael Porter together, you have to admit Michael Porter has to be under suspicion. Beth was close to him. Real cosy. If you get my meaning. I wouldn't be surprised if he was behind it all. He seemed nice enough, earnest enough, sincere enough, but as Daddy says, they're often the worst sort.

Are you taking any pictures for this piece? Let me just fix my hair...

Michael Porter

I didn't think she'd do it. I mean, yes, we talked about making Howard Johnson take notice, about doing something significant. But I didn't think she took me seriously. I mean she's a school-girl. I nearly died when she told me who her parents were. I mean they were huge in the No Dams days (they were chained to the trees, went to jail) the Greens owe them a great deal. I know Benny Black is God, but Grace and Roger were constant: their commitment is legendary. Being in parliament is one thing but it's people like Grace and Roger that make us strong. She never stops *actually* helping people in a *practical* sense and his legal practice does huge things for the movement. How could this girl be theirs??

To be truthful, I *was* flattered. Well, Bethany is a most attractive girl. Yes, you could say beautiful, and yes I was attracted to her. But that's all – no more than a normal male appreciation of an attractive young woman. She wanted to be helpful. She said she was ready to come of age politically and she wanted a different view to her parents. She wasn't convinced that their politics should be hers. But when I pointed out to her that the state of the forests was more her concern than her parents because of the impact so few trees would have on her future she began to see that she needed to know more. After all she was turning 18. She was about to be an adult – she was very aware of this. So we discussed the immigration policies, how barbarically the detainees were treated. How reprehensible it was for a country like ours to be so intolerant and cruel to people so clearly in need.

Bethany was about to vote and she wanted

to make a difference. She wanted to know all about our democratic system; the ins and outs, the wonderful beauty of it all, not just the election day brouhaha. What politician wouldn't want a young person like that around?

She was very excited about the Youth Parliament. The chance to be in the State Chamber and debate serious issues like real politicians. It was good that she believed that politicians were there to do good. I know I am. But some of the others, well… It's simple really, they've been there far too long and they're only worried about staying elected and their pension.

I tried not to influence her opinion on our great leaders. But, like a child she asked very simple but difficult questions. *If we're such a rich country why don't we have free education and better hospitals? If the economy is booming how come so many people live in poverty? Why can't the Prime Minister say Sorry to the Aboriginal people? Why doesn't anyone in federal cabinet get sacked when they fuck up?*

Johnson has to go. It's simple. But through normal democratic means. I explained this to Bethany. That the attraction of the West for those poor detainees and refugees was our democracy, where people vote without fear to elect a government that can be voted out again, not in power for life or with the military running the place. I'm not sure that she really understands the intricacies of democracy. I think she was too overwhelmed by the lies and corruption. That she felt my own despair about this and my own fear that

I too might succumb to *the dark side* in order to remain in parliament. I would rather die than betray my constituents or my beliefs. Bethany said that she wished Howard Johnson had the moral and ethical integrity that I had, that she truly admired me and could never see how it would be possible for me to end up as corrupt and weak as him.

It's true, we talked at length about democracy and corruption, that despite all the problems with our politicans and parliament we still have it so much better than many other countries. She said I needed to stop being complacent, that accepting *good enough* wasn't good enough. I could see her point. She wanted a democracy that worked for all, not just the few. She was appaled at the influence of lobby groups, of key individuals who had such immense behind the scenes power. She was enraged. Perhaps I shouldn't have shared so much of the behind the scenes machinations that oil the wheels of politics. Perhaps I spoke to her like a mature adult when she was/is really a child grappling with challenging and difficult ideas. But she listened so intently and asked such difficult and insightful questions. How could I not be entranced by her?

It's true, we talked about what she might say to Howard Johnson at the conclusion of the National Youth Parliament. I was impressed by the change in her from the beginnings of her political journey, from those first bills for the local YP to how polished and accomplished she was in her preparations for Canberra. I could see her as a future MP. Her passion, her commitment was wonderful to behold and yes, I felt proud of my role in her development. Roger even told me that he was pleased to see Bethany so energised about something that mattered. I felt a sense of relief in him that she'd found her calling.

I thought she was simply going to talk to Johnson. Get him alone and give him a piece of her mind. That's what I thought she was going to do. Impress him with her youth and passion and try to make a change that way.

You need to understand that I did *not* incite Bethany to do anything. I am not a violent man. I believe in the democratic principles of our government and support the people's right to choose, even when I think they're wrong. I am a pacifist. I've never been in a fight in my life. Not even as a schoolboy. I promise you, that's true. I am simply a passionate man, willing to fight through words and non-violent deeds to make this a better country. I'm sorry Bethany misunderstood me.

Thank you.

Sylvia Johansen

I simply cannot talk to you, young man. You should realise that. I am not in a position to speak about this matter at all. The headmaster has released a statement, perhaps I could read that to you?

"*The Headmaster and Board deeply regret the recent incident between Bethany Tyler and the Honourable Prime Minister. We wish to make it clear that the school does not*

*support violence, or aggressive actions in
any shape or form. The school categorically
denies any involvement with Bethany Tyler's
actions. Her behaviour does not reflect the
educational principles or standards offered
at our school. We send our best wishes to
the Prime Minister for a speedy and full
recovery."*

Bethany Tyler

I guess you're after some sort of scoop. Any
sort of financial inducement to talk to you
as opposed to anyone else? You know *Sixty
Minutes* has offered a very tidy sum for an
exclusive. So, I'm not sure about talking to
you at all.
  Ah, I see … Let's begin then.
  You need to understand that there's an
awful lot of bullshit around this. I'm
reading the papers, even in here, and there's
lots of rubbish being written about me. And
really it's very simple. Howard Johnson is
the worst prime minister this country has
ever had. He had to go. Simple.
  This is the most reactive, anti-
Indigenous, anti-migrant, anti-woman, anti-
student, anti-worker government this country
has *ever* seen. Only the rich and privileged
are safe – are protected! And they don't need
it! What happened to the idea of the
government looking after the people? Of
making sure we have decent public education
and health care? Of treating refugees with
compassion, not suspicion and not locking
them up and throwing away their futures. Have
you been to Baxter? Have you seen the

pictures, talked to any of the people? What about remote Australia? Have you seen the squalor our Indigenous people live in? What's your paper doing about it? Why not an expose of the third world conditions rife there? I'm not the story, they are.

Politics suck. Democracy is a crock of shit. They're all corrupt and fucking each other. I wouldn't even spit on the federal opposition. They're no better than those self satisfied smug pricks on the government benches. The Greens are the future. Greens and Independents. I couldn't vote for anyone else. You should see how hard Michael works. Michael Porter, the member for Mottling in the State Legislative Assembly. A devoted and dedicated prince of a man. He should be PM. He has more integrity in his little finger than all of those men and women – well perhaps not Natasha or Julia - in Canberra. I tell you he should be running the country. Then I'd be proud to be Australian again. A country of integrity and compassion, where social justice really matters. Where people, not profit, are what matters. And trees stay put as things of beauty and necessity for the health of the planet.

I had no choice, you understand. I *had* to do something. So when I was chosen after the Youth Parliament to go to Canberra with some of the others I jumped at it. Mum and Dad were pleased as. Michael was proud too. I am his protégé after all. No matter what's happened, and how he denies me, it was for him.

It was a simple plan. Get close. Get violent. Who would suspect a schoolgirl? And one as Anglo and well presented as myself. I mean, you should see me in my uniform with my shiny blonde hair in its precise pony tail, set off by long pins in the school colours. Yes, the epitome of G-rated, as my brother, Will, would say. I looked innocent and earnest and I was most honoured to be introduced to Mr Howard Johnson. And then to have him engage in conversation! Totally trivial and patronising, of course. But what could you expect? He *is* such a busy and important man. Even a silly little schoolgirl – who was almost voting age – knew that.

And it *was* planned. I thought it all through. Not from the moment I met Michael, but from the moment we knew we were going to Canberra. There would be a reception for us after the National Youth Parliament wound up. We'd all go up to the Governor General's House and be feted: the PM would be there and make a speech. So I knew I had the opportunity to get close. But to do what and how? So I thought for some time; knew there'd be security, knew I needed something sharp. Could I smuggle something in, or get hold of a knife in there? What to do? One of my friends at school, who, yes is a boy but *not* my boyfriend, makes amazing things in metalwork. So I asked him to make me some bespoke hair pins – they're just like chop sticks and we stick them throguh our pony tails or use them to bundle our hair on our heads in a messy bun-thing. Metal ones, in the school colours, for when I went away, nice and sharp too. He raised his eye-brows at that but I kissed him and he blushed and said *for you, Beth, anything*. And no, he didn't have a clue what I was going to do, so don't go visiting him.

So I had my weapons but knew they'd cause a problem with security. I knew I'd have to devise some sort of diversionary activity, or rely on people under-estimating me, because I'm *just a school-girl* after all. But I'm not a *silly* schoolgirl. I am a political activist with metal weapons in my hair. So much for the security at Parliament House. Or precisely, the security men. I had a moment of nerves at this juncture, but the security men behaved almost as scripted in my fantasy plan: taken in by my appearance, my demeanour of innocence. All I had to do was smile and say, *Oh, but they're just decorations, so my hair looks nice. It's so important for your hair to look nice. You must look your best on such important occasions.* So they smiled back, nodded, stared too blatantly at my tits and passed me through. And I got my chance. But he barely gave me the time of day. He was too busy fobbing me off, treating me like the security men. As he turned away from me, I pulled my blue, black and silver steel decorations from my pony tail, *stumbled* into him and thrust them both up under his arm pit, into that bit where seams can be weak on suits and the flesh is yielding and bleeds quickly and might possibly come close to an organ or two.

He cried out immediately: like a stuck pig, bellowing in pain. I stood back, pulled my weapons away, wiping them quickly on the nearby tablecloth before putting them back in my hair, as he fell to the floor with a great crash, blood soaking his chest. People rushed around, looking frantic and stupid. *Who did this?* Someone screamed. *Get an ambulance!* Another shouted. *Room – give him room. Get these children out. Now*! Orders flying all over the place and I was hustled out of the room with the others. While they looked in all the wrong places. So much for all their supposed readiness for a terror attack: *I* was reassured by what I saw that afternoon in our capital. *Not.*

But Howard Johnson didn't die. He isn't dead yet, although I believe he hovers between this world and the next. I'm not sure that I wanted that anyway. After all that would cement his name in history. I just wanted to hurt him, for him to know how much he was hurting so many of us. I wanted him to feel the pain of so many Australians. That was what I wanted. He needs to feel pain, to suffer.

Then, when we were all called in for questioning, even though it would have been easy to lie and deny it – they'd already arrested some poor Iranian guy who worked in the kitchens – I wanted Johnson to know who did it. I wanted him to know I wasn't just a silly girl who could be dismissed with a non-answer and a wave of his hand. I am a citizen about to vote for the first time. And. I. Care.

They didn't know what to do. They didn't believe me. It wasn't until I handed over my hair-sticks, with some residual bits of blood and flesh (which went off for testing) that they released the poor kitchen-hand and walked me off to the police station with Mrs Johansen frantically making calls to anyone who might be able to help.

Yes, I admit it. I wanted Michael to see what I was made of. To show him that I was worthy. That he may be over thirty and I'm not quite eighteen but I can be his equal. I am as capable as him, or Grace, of making a difference to this nation. I can change things, make people take notice. You know I can, or you wouldn't be here. You see how long I'm in the news for. You watch. I'll have book and movie deals coming out my ears. It won't matter how long they jail me for. It won't matter if Howard Johnson lives or dies. My future is certain. My place in history is assured. Kids will read about *me* in History lessons in years to come.

You make sure you tell Michael, when you talk to him. Tell him it was because of him, it was for him, and he should call me. He could be a big part of the story. He could be the romantic lead. Yes, tell him, the romantic lead.

I guess you want pictures too?

THE END

About the author

Jackie Swift has been a better than average English teacher for all of her working life, running successful English Departments across the world, doing her best to foster a love of reading and writing in her teenage charges; sometimes even succeeding!

She's accumulated an excess of degrees over the years, including a PhD: in Creative Writing. She won her first prize for writing aged 10 and has been writing ever since: publishing articles, short stories and poetry; winning the odd small prize along the way, as well as publishing some dubious erotica under a very much assumed name.

You can follow her on Twitter @jactherat

About Fahrenzine

Fahrenzine is a new adventure in publishing brought to you exclusively by Fahrenheit Press.

Each issue features a single short story from one of the most exciting crime fiction talents in the world and is limited to only 100 hand-numbered copies.

Fahrenzine takes inspiration from our old skool punk heritage and pays homage to the pioneering DIY spirit of revolutionary zines like Sniffin Glue, Chainsaw and New York Rocker.

Submissions are open and stories must be between 5000-7000 words long.

If you think you've got what it takes, send your submissions to:

fahrenzine@fahrenheit-press.com

Printed in Great Britain
by Amazon